System Shock

Liam O'Donnell

Illustrated by Janek Matysiak

A & C Black · London

To Mom who let me play D & D.
To Gerrie who gave me a home while I wrote this story.
To Aileen who got my stories read to her entire class.

L.O'D.

If you want to write to the author of 'System Shock'
you can email him at: <u>odonnellliam@hotmail.com</u>

Chapter One

The year is 2115 A.D. The computer network known as the System is linked to Earth, often called Realworld, within the web of Cyberspace. Daniel Banner and his best friend Jack Needles are tapped into the Virtual Reality world of the System, to play their favourite VR game, *Shadow War*.

Daniel stuck his head through the program rip and saw the tall Infoblocks of the System under its skin of programming. 'Each one of those towers holds billions of bytes of information,' he gasped. 'It's beautiful.'

Jack was at his shoulder, staring in awe.

Chapter Two

On the ground, far below the towering Infoblocks, Jemma Roden raced through the System at a bit-blurring pace, hunting for hidden data.

C'mon Jemma, report back. You've been in there a long time.

Relax, Statto. I'm just enjoying the scenery.

Yeah, well the client is getting a bit nervous...

Tell that info-hungry blimp to cool his hard drive. I know what I'm doing.

Suddenly a nearby Infoblock exploded, splitting the normally church-like silence of the System with a deafening roar and blinding light. The impact of digital rubble knocked Jemma from her Circuitbike.

Statto, come in, Statto.
Do you read me?

Jemma's com-link was silent.

Must have been
damaged in the crash.

Her ride destroyed, cut off from the Realworld,
Jemma was alone in the System.

15

From the darkness a terrifying beast, half bear, half owl, jumped in front of Daniel and Jemma. They watched in wonder as the giant Owlbear sent the Pigkin flying with a vicious blend of martial arts and a hefty oak staff.

The strange Owlbear scooped Daniel and Jemma in its arms. 'Hold on, little chicks,' he said as they disappeared into the darkness, leaving the dazed Pigkin behind.

Thax nodded and scratched his beak.

That is correct Daniel.
Now I'm here to help you save the System.
Azkar, the evil SpellSinger, from the *Shadow War* game has escaped from his program and has seized control of the entire System Core by releasing every villain from every VR game.

That's why I can't contact Realworld on my com-link.

'Why has he cut off communication with Realworld?' asked Daniel.
'So that he can enter it himself,' Thax whispered. He could barely be heard over the howling and yelping of the computer beasts running wild above them.

23

25

Thax swung his oak staff at one of the DataHound's drooling jaws. It caught the end neatly and crunched loudly. When Thax yanked the staff back its tip was gone. 'Whatever they bite they erase!' he shouted.

Jemma! She's abandoned us!

Better think of something, Daniel! I'm running out of staff and they look hungry!

Chapter Four

'The next bite will finish the staff,' Thax called over the loud growls of the DataHounds. 'After that, they're chewing feathers. Get ready to run!'

Daniel searched for an escape route. Darkness lay around them.

'Run where?' he asked, but Thax did not answer.

From the darkness above the bridge Jemma hovered down in a Cybersled, a wry smile on her face.

Thax tossed the DataHounds the remains of his staff. They devoured it hungrily. He and Daniel jumped in the Cybersled. Jemma punched the controls.

Anyone need a lift?

The Cybersled launched into the air leaving the confused DataHounds behind. 'It's mob rule all through the System,' Jemma explained. 'So I just borrowed the Cybersled from some unsuspecting alien-types.'

'Those DataHounds were Azkar's beasts.' Thax said. 'He'll be waiting for us at the Core.'
'Somehow, I don't think he'll be putting out the *Welcome* mat,' Daniel sighed heavily.

Soon Jemma set the Cybersled down in a niche in the digital landscape.

The Core is just over this slope.

31

At the top of the slope, an army of evil villains guarded the System Core.

33

'This is a DataWeaver.' Thax spoke like a school teacher. 'DataHounds devour the digital information that makes up the System but DataWeavers spin the data, creating new information.'

'A digital life-cycle,' Daniel said, amazed. The System was much more than a place to play VR games. It was an ecosystem all in itself.

'How is this little guy going to help us get into the Core?' Jemma asked.

Like this.

Daniel froze as Thax placed the large hairy DataWeaver on top of his head.
'The DataWeaver will spin data around us so that we don't stand out so much.'

A disguise!

'Anything you want, but remember we have to look like the thugs down there,' Thax warned.

Make him *one of those* Pig-men, DataWeaver!

'I want to be Danno Vile Mouth, my VR character from *Shadow War*,' Daniel said. The DataWeaver set to work spinning him a digital disguise.

The DataWeaver set to work on both of them, spinning the disguises of their choice. With its work done, it slipped back into Thax's satchel and they were ready to wade through the sea of computer villains.

Chapter Six

The army of video-game evil had set up a makeshift town of campfires and stalls selling everything from medieval weapons to high-tech digital upgrades. Thax, Daniel and Jemma abandoned the Cybersled when the crowds got too thick. Soon they were in the thick of the mass of monsters, walking down a narrow street that led to the giant System Core. This was no place for polite manners. Pushing and shoving was the only way to move ahead.

Hey, watch where you're stompin', bird-brain!

Eat steel, Pork-face!

After much elbowing and foot-stomping they reached a set of large, wooden double doors.
'This must be the entrance to the Core,' Thax said.
The doors had no handles to turn or knockers to bang.

'I am Olaf, the Gatekeeper', the tiny, smelly man said with pride. 'To get through those doors you must defeat me in single combat.'

Daniel flexed his abundant muscles proudly.

'Very well, halfling, I won't hurt you too bad,' he boasted loudly to the growing crowd of onlookers. 'I will leave you in one piece, so that you can still open the doors for us.'

He gripped his sword tighter, stepping closer to the little man.

43

The crowd of monsters cheered loudly, moving in closer when Olaf finished his transformation. The game had begun and there was nowhere to run.

Chapter Seven

There's nothing we can do. If we try and help him the crowd will attack us.

Daniel, alone, had to defeat the beast to get into the Core. He quickly dodged Olaf's swiping claw. One hit with those razor-sharp blades and he'd be finished. He soon realised he was no match for the monster, muscles or no muscles.

Can't beat him with strength. Got to use my brain.

Daniel dodged left, then right, narrowly escaping Olaf's claws each time. He was getting tired and time was running out. The more Olaf attacked him, however, the more Daniel felt that he'd seen the beast before. Between dodges, he frantically searched the depths of his mind, trying to retrieve some piece of knowledge buried there. Then, like locating a missing program file, the answer appeared, refusing to be ignored.

The jewel!

47

Daniel brandished the stone over the defeated ShapeShifter. Wagers, won or lost, were exchanged as the bloodthirsty crowd wandered away, grumbling with disappointment. Without his precious jewel Olaf had melted to his halfling shape.

'It is not often I come up against brains and brawn,' he said, sheepishly. 'You may proceed.'

Now the real challenge begins.

Chapter Eight

Inside the Core was pitch black. Thax conjured up light to guide them.

'We appear to be inside some ancient tomb,' Thax whispered. His voice echoed off the stone walls.

Hmm... We had a history disk about Egypt at school, ages ago. Those pictures on the wall must be hieroglyphics. I wonder what they say?

'Probably "This place is spooky. Get out while you still can!"' Daniel said, sticking close to the comforting ball of light.

The stone walls shook wildly, sending large rocks falling from the ceiling into the darkness below. From the ledge across the cavern a bridge pushed outward and inched its way to Thax and Daniel. It butted into their side with a resounding thud. Jemma appeared at the far side.

'Hurry,' she called. 'The bridge will retract in a few seconds.'
Thax and Daniel ran across the narrow stone path, high above the cavern floor.

'We learned at school that the Egyptians filled their tombs with secrets and traps, to stop robbers.' Jemma explained. 'The lever triggered the bridge.'
'Who would have thought school would save our lives?' Daniel said.

Chapter Nine

Daniel shook his head, trying to let his eyes adjust to the bright lights that twinkled round the large room.

Azkar!

Welcome, Realworlder.

The evil Spellsinger's voice was slow and thick like honey oozing down a knife edge. 'I'm afraid you are too late to save your companion. I have his Guide-chip and will be leaving this wretched System very soon.'

'Do not worry about your friend,' Azkar continued. 'I've taken good care of him. You could say I've been a father to him.' He giggled. Daniel was too scared to see what was so funny. 'I call him Borg.'

Out of the shadows the massive shape of the Borg thumped. All three of them gasped in unison when they saw the human body cruelly mixed with machinery to create a demonic blend of man and machine: a Cyborg.

Chapter Ten

The entire System rocked under the power of the DatWipe. Jemma scrambled to keep on her feet when the violent tremors hit. Programmers in Realworld were deleting the very space they were in, one data line at a time. Solid walls seemed to vanish. At first they showed their graphic structure and then disappeared completely.

Now it appears you have a choice, my friends: either be devoured by my pets or let your friends in Realworld delete you. I really wish I could stay and watch but I must be getting on my way. Bye, bye!

Thax and Jemma huddled together as the DataHounds slowly moved in.

'Azkar plans to use the chaos of the DatWipe as a cover when he slips into your world!' Thax said as he swung his vicious blade at the nearest beast. It dodged the blade easily, enjoying the fighting spirit of its next meal.

'We have to stop him from linking with Jack's Guide-chip,' Jemma said.

The inky black dogs snarled, waiting for the right moment to pounce. Jemma cracked her whip into the darkness above and launched herself at the DataHounds.

Jemma rushed at Azkar, jumping over data-holes that yawned open at her feet as the floor was deleted. Despite his withered appearance, the old wizard turned with lightning speed, a thick, gummy web shooting from his fingertips.

Why don't you stick around, my dear?

Jemma collapsed under the gooey weight. With every touch, the webbing ate away at her DataWeaver's disguise, and tightened its sticky grip. Around her the System Core crumbled as the DatWipe reached full force.

Thax was trapped under the two fierce DataHounds, his feathery arms and legs starting to vanish as they devoured his programming.

Faster and faster the data-holes appeared in the walls around him. This time the DataHounds had no interest in Thax's staff. Leaping with blinding speed the evil hounds pounced at the Owlbear, deleting his digital being with every cruel bite.

Daniel watched in horror as everything fell apart: Jemma fell under Azkar's spell and Thax fought with the vicious DataHounds, the System crumbling around him. His eyes left the Borg for only a second but that was all the machine-man needed. Two metal claws pierced Daniel's thick armour and sunk towards his skin.

Chapter Eleven

Jack's stolen Guide-chip snapped into place on Azkar's wrinkled neck.

I must slip into the DatWipe stream at just the right moment. Too soon or too late means instant death.

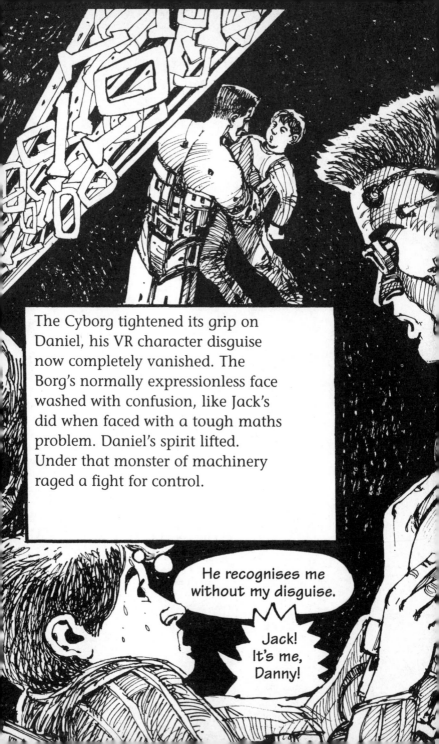

The Cyborg's expression changed once more and quietly a single word came from its mouth, 'Lardbelly'. 'Don't call me Lardbelly!' Daniel yelled, then changed his mind. 'Call me whatever you like! It's just good to have you back, Jack.'
He felt a rush of relief when Jack, now in complete control of his monstrous machine body, set him down on the ground.

Azkar has your Guide-chip!

Jack bore down on the old wizard, vengeance running through his circuits.

Azkar didn't hear Jack's lumbering steps behind him. but he defintely felt it when the Cyborg tore the Guide-chip from his neck.

Too stunned to let off a spell, Azkar flailed like a rag doll when Jack scooped him up.

Silence filled the empty chamber. Their surroundings stopped deleting, as if someone had hit a pause button. Then the System Core glowed warmly, like a machine newly repaired.

The blast must have re-connected us to Realworld!

CONNECTION·MADE·SYSTEM·ONLINE

From the void of deleted data, hundreds of DataWeavers crawled, the clicking of their legs sounding like a computer rebooting itself. They set to work rebuilding the System, weaving the data that held it together, one program line at time.